This book belongs to

. . . .

First published in 2014 by Miles Kelly Publishing Ltd
Harding's Barn, Bardfield End Green, Thaxted, Essex, CM6 3PX, UK

2 4 6 8 10 9 7 5 3 1

Publishing Director Belinda Gallagher
Creative Director Jo Cowan
Editor Fran Bromage
Senior Designer Joe Jones
Production Manager Elizabeth Collins
Reprographics Stephan Davis, Jennifer Hunt, Thom Allaway

ISBN 978-1-78209-492-0

Printed in China

British Library Cataloguing-in-Publication Data
A catalogue record for this book is available from the British Library

ACKNOWLEDGEMENTS

The publishers would like to thank the following artists
who have contributed to this book:
Cover (main): Hannah Wood at Advocate Art
Insides: Pam Smy

Made with paper from a sustainable forest

www.mileskelly.net info@mileskelly.net

Aladdin

Miles Kelly

Aladdin and his mother were very poor. One day, a merchant arrived. He said he was Aladdin's uncle and offered Aladdin work.

Aladdin

Together, they went out into the burning-hot desert. Aladdin's uncle built a fire and scattered strange-smelling powders into it. There was a big burst of smoke and a small trapdoor appeared in the earth.

Story time

"Go down and find me an old lamp!" shouted the uncle. Aladdin was frozen with fear. "Go!" yelled the man, handing him a ring. "This magic ring will keep you safe!"

Aladdin walked down into deep, dark caves until he

reached a beautiful garden. The trees sparkled with glass fruits, and Aladdin couldn't resist filling his pockets.

Then Aladdin spotted a rusty lamp lying on the grass. He took it back to his uncle, who barked, "Give it to me!"

but Aladdin was suspicious. "Help me out first," he replied.

Aladdin was right to be wary, for the merchant was really an evil sorcerer. When Aladdin refused to give him the lamp, he pushed Aladdin back down into the cave and

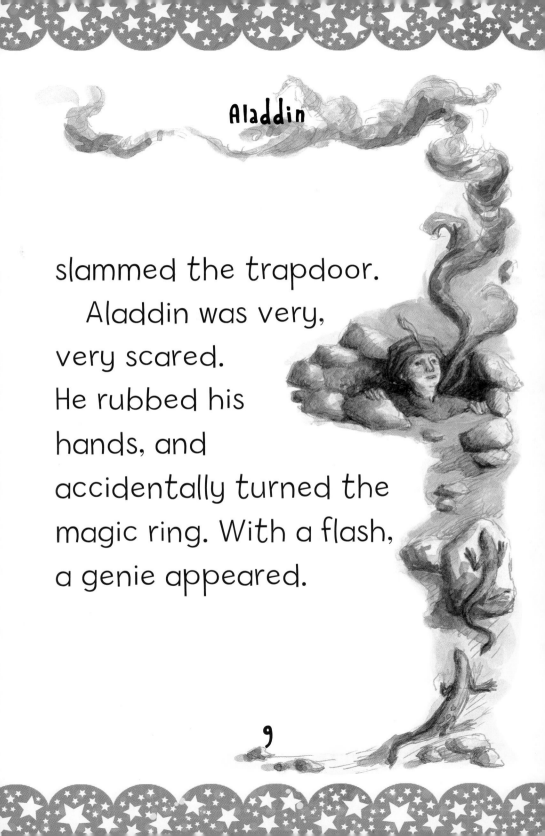

slammed the trapdoor.
Aladdin was very,
very scared.
He rubbed his
hands, and
accidentally turned the
magic ring. With a flash,
a genie appeared.

9

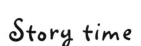
Story time

"I am the genie of the ring!"
the genie said. "Speak a wish
O master and I will obey."
Aladdin wished he was out
of the cave. Suddenly he
found himself back at home.
He showed his mother the
glass fruits and the old lamp.

Aladdin

"I'll clean the lamp up a bit," said Aladdin, and he gave it a rub with his sleeve. There was another blinding flash, and an even bigger genie appeared.

"I am the genie of the lamp!" it roared. "Speak a wish

O master and I will obey."
Aladdin asked for something to eat, and a huge table appeared laden with delicious food on golden platters.

Aladdin

After that, the lives of Aladdin and his mother changed completely. They were careful not to arouse suspicion though, and only sold a few golden platters.

Then, one day Aladdin saw a great procession and he

caught sight of the beautiful Princess Balroubadour. From then on, Aladdin couldn't speak, eat, or sleep, he was so much in love.

Aladdin's mother watched him getting thinner every day. One day, she packed up

the golden platters and the
sparkling, coloured glass
fruits and went to see the
princess's father, the Sultan.

The Sultan immediately
realized that the glass fruits
were precious jewels. He
hoped Aladdin would have

more, so he agreed Aladdin could marry his daughter.

That night Aladdin risked using the lamp to wish for a splendid palace. The wedding was held the next

Aladdin

day, and Aladdin and his
bride were very happy.
   A few months later,
when Aladdin was out,
a peddler came through
the streets shouting, "New
lamps for old!" The princess's
maid handed over Aladdin's

old lamp. As soon as the lamp was in the peddler's hands he gave a cry of delight and vanished. Seconds later, the princess, her maid and the palace disappeared too!

When Aladdin returned he realized that the sorcerer

Aladdin

had taken the princess. He
quickly turned the magic ring
he always wore and asked to
be taken to his missing wife.

"The sorcerer has gone
out," the princess said, when
Aladdin appeared beside her,
"we must find the lamp."

19

Quickly, Aladdin mixed a sleeping powder into a goblet of wine. He had just enough time to hide before the

sorcerer returned. Princess Balroubadour

20

Aladdin

rushed to offer the sorcerer the refreshing drink. As soon as he had drained the whole goblet, he crumpled to the floor and began to snore.

Aladdin found the lamp in the sorcerer's coat, rubbed it quickly and gave the order.

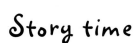

Story time

In a puff of smoke, Aladdin, the princess and the palace were all back safely. "I give you your freedom!" he told the genie, and the overjoyed genie was gone forever.

Aladdin and his princess lived happily ever after, and

when the sorcerer woke up,
he got what he had always
wanted — a rusty
old lamp!

The End